THE CHRISTMAS TEDDY BEAR

BY JENNIFER JORDAN
ILLUSTRATED BY STEPHANIE RYDER

Brimax . Newmarket . England

Bobby Bear lived by himself in the forest. It was Christmas Eve but Bobby Bear was unhappy. His house was old and very cold. There were holes in the roof and some of the windows were broken.

"This house is falling down," said Bobby Bear. "I must find somewhere nice to live for Christmas."

He packed his clothes and his
toothbrush and began his search
for a new home. It started to
snow.
"I must find a new home soon,"
said Bobby Bear.
Rosie Robin flew down beside
him.
"You can share my nest until
Spring," she said.
"Thank you, Rosie," said Bobby,
"But I am far too big."

Bobby Bear saw a little house in the bushes.

"Hello," he said. "I am looking for somewhere to live."

"I live here with my five children," said Poppy Fox. "Gertie Goose lives all alone. You should try there. If you go straight ahead and turn left at the big tree you will come to a bridge. You should see Gertie's house from there."

"Thank you," said Bobby.

It began to snow harder and Bobby Bear couldn't remember whether he should have turned left or right at the tree. He saw a house and knocked on the door.

"Can you tell me where Gertie Goose's house is?" he asked.

"Turn left here," said Ben Rabbit, "until you come to the bridge. You will see Gertie's house from there."

"Thank you," said Bobby.

Bobby Bear turned left but the snow started to fall heavily. Bobby could not see where he was going. He could not find the bridge. He was lost.

"Oh no!" said Bobby. "It is very cold and I have nowhere to live, I cannot find Gertie Goose's house. What am I going to do?"

Bobby continued walking, hoping that he would find the bridge soon.

It began to get dark. Bobby Bear walked on feeling very cold and very tired. Then, under the fir trees, he saw the biggest house he had ever seen. It had candles in the windows and a big Christmas tree by the door.

"What a lovely house," said Bobby Bear. "This is where I would like to stay for Christmas."

The door was open and Bobby Bear walked inside. No one seemed to be at home. Bobby Bear looked around. There were toys everywhere. He saw train sets, puzzles and toy cars. There were dolls, games and books. There was even a big rocking-horse. The house was just full of toys.

Bobby Bear was very tired so he sat on a sofa in front of the fire.

"Don't you know who lives here?" said a little mouse, who lived under the sofa.

"No, I don't," said Bobby Bear in a sleepy voice.

"Santa lives here," said the little mouse.

But Bobby Bear said nothing. He was fast asleep!

That night, Santa filled his sleigh with toys and gave his reindeer a big supper. Bobby Bear was still fast asleep. Santa picked him up and put him on the sleigh next to three dolls and a big toy rabbit. It was still snowing as they set off through the forest to deliver the toys.

At her house, Gertie Goose hung her stocking by her bed. Poppy Fox and her babies hung their stocking on the door. At his house, Ben Rabbit and his brothers and sisters hung a little sack beside the Christmas tree. They were very excited when they went to bed, but they were all fast asleep when Santa crept into their houses with their presents.

Soon it was Christmas morning and Bobby Bear woke up after his long sleep.

"Where am I?" he said, looking all around him.

He was in a Christmas stocking by Gertie Goose's bed. Gertie woke up.

"How lovely!" she cried. "Santa has left a teddy bear in my stocking!"

Bobby Bear kept very still as Gertie gave him a big hug.

Gertie's friends arrived for her party.

"Merry Christmas!" said Gertie. "Look at my lovely teddy bear." But Bobby Bear's nose started to tickle.

"Atishoo!" he sneezed.

"Teddy bears cannot sneeze!" said Poppy Fox.

"It's me!" said Bobby Bear. "I fell asleep in Santa's house and he thought I was a teddy bear!"

The party was over and Gertie's house was very quiet.

"What a lovely party," said Bobby Bear.

Gertie had learned that Bobby Bear had no home.

"You can live with me now," she said. "I have a spare room and I get lonely by myself."

"Thank you, Gertie," said Bobby Bear. "Santa has given both of us a present. You have a new friend and I have a new home."

Say these words again.

lived	forest
clothes	toothbrush
house	bushes
snow	harder
somewhere	friends
began	dark
spare	present